Three Pebbles and a Song

Eileen Spinelli

pictures by S. D. Schindler

DIAL BOOKS FOR YOUNG READERS ◈ NEW YORK

Published by Dial Books for Young Readers

A division of Penguin Putnam Inc.

345 Hudson Street

New York, New York 10014

Text copyright © 2003 by Eileen Spinelli

Pictures copyright © 2003 by S. D. Schindler

Designed by Atha Tehon

Text set in Breughel

Manufactured in China on acid-free paper

1 3 5 7 9 10 8 6 4 2

Library of Congress Cataloging-in-Publication Data

Spinelli, Eileen.

Three pebbles and a song / Eileen Spinelli ; pictures by S. D. Schindler.

p. cm.

Summary: As his mouse family endures a long, cold winter, Moses's contributions
of a dance, a juggling act, and a little song prove more useful than he had supposed.

ISBN 0-8037-2528-0

[1. Mice—Fiction. 2. Winter—Fiction.] I. Schindler, S. D., ill.

II.Title.

PZ7.S7566 Sk 2003 [E]—dc21 2002006822

The art was prepared using gouache, watercolors,
colored inks, pastels, and chalk on marbelized paper.

For the Bryants—Jen, Neil and Leigh
E.S.

To the Mouse Lady of Hyde Park
S.D.S.

Across the moonlit fields crackly old leaves twirled and skittered.
And so did Moses.

As he danced, his mama came bustling by.
"What are you doing, Moses?" Mama asked.
"I'm twirling and skittering," said Moses.

"Snow's coming," Mama sighed. "We need food.
Warm things for the nest. Gathering's best."
So Moses set off to gather.

But as the wind *shicka-whished* through the papery stalks of corn, Moses couldn't resist joining in its whistle-y song.

As he sang, his papa came hurrying by.
"What are you doing, Moses?" Papa asked.

"I'm singing and humming a whistle-y song," said Moses.
"Snow's coming," Papa squealed. "We need food. Warm
things for the nest. Gathering's best."
So Moses set off to gather.

A patch of pebbles gleamed beside the creek. Pebbles were not food.
They would not keep a nest warm.
But Moses couldn't resist picking one up.

Moses tossed the pebble into the air. He caught it! Moses picked up another pebble. He tossed both. He caught them! Then . . . three pebbles up in the air!

Catch-a-toss-catch.

His sister, Missy, came scurrying by.
"What are you doing, Moses?" Missy asked.
"I'm tossing and catching. Catching and tossing," said Moses.

"Snow's coming," Missy yipped. "We need food.
Warm things for the nest. Gathering's best."

Snow came. Thick and fast it fell and fell.

Moses scampered back to the nest.

Mama was there. She had gathered an apronful of crumbs.
Papa was there. He had gathered four soft rags and a sackful of corn.
Missy was there. She had gathered five raisins.
But Moses had gathered only a dance, a song, and three
gleaming pebbles.

Ever so slowly, the wintry days and nights passed.
Outside, the snow lay cold and deep.
But thanks to Papa's soft rags, the nest was warm.
Thanks to his corn and Mama's crumbs, there was plenty to eat.
And thanks to Missy's raisins, there was even something sweet for
special occasions—such as Papa's birthday and Be Nice to Mice Day.

"In fact," said Papa, "life would be just about perfect
  if only we weren't so . . ."

"So what?" Moses asked.

"Bored," Mama sighed.

"Bored stiff," squealed Papa.

"Bored to tears," yipped Missy.

"When I'm bored," Moses said, "look what I do!"

He pulled the three pebbles from his pocket.
Catch-a-toss-catch.
Everyone *clap-clap-clapped*.

Then Moses sang a whistle-y song that sounded like wind
through the corn.
Everyone *cheer-cheer-cheered*.

Then Moses began to twirl and to skitter.
He grabbed Missy by the hand.
Then Missy grabbed Mama,
and Mama joined hands with Papa.
Skitter and twirl, twirl and skitter.
Together they danced round and round.
Before long everyone was giggling
and out of breath.

And ever after, all snowy season long, the words
"I am bored" were never heard again.
Missy juggled corn.

Papa sang a song that sounded like snow
creaking on the roof. Mama spun and dipped.
In fact, everyone was having such a good time that
Moses was the only one who noticed . . .

when spring arrived!